JANNETTE LAROCHE

MINNEAPOLIS

Darby Creek
A division of Lerner Publishing Group, Inc.
241 First Avenue North
Minneapolis, MN 55401 USA

For reading levels and more information, look up this title at www.lernerbooks.com.

Image credits: Irina_QQQ/Shutterstock.com (puzzle); Anucha Cheechang/Shutterstock.com (clock); Nina_Lisitsyna/Shutterstock.com (digital).

Main body text set in Janson Text LT Std 12/17.5.
Typeface provided by Adobe Systems.

Library of Congress Cataloging-in-Publication Data

Names: LaRoche, Jannette, author.
Title: Escape! / Jannette LaRoche.
Description: Minneapolis : Darby Creek, [2019] | Series: Reality show | Summary: Best friends Hendrix, Kane, Raymon, and Ander team up on a televised escape room competition, but when tensions run high and confrontations occur, more than the prize money is at risk.
Identifiers: LCCN 2018027164 (print) | LCCN 2018034935 (ebook) | ISBN 9781541541900 (eb pdf) | ISBN 9781541540279 (lb : alk. paper) | ISBN 9781541545410 (pb : alk. paper)
Subjects: | CYAC: Escapes (Amusements)—Fiction. | Reality television programs—Fiction. | Best friends—Fiction. | Friendship—Fiction. | Cooperativeness—Fiction.
Classification: LCC PZ7.1.L355 (ebook) | LCC PZ7.1.L355 Esc 2019 (print) | DDC [Fic]—dc23

LC record available at https://lccn.loc.gov/2018027164

Manufactured in the United States of America
1-45232-36614-9/11/2018

For Chris, Nico, and Raimi

CHAPTER 1

Hendrix ducked as an arrow whizzed past his head, missing by mere millimeters. He yelled and dove behind a barrel to check his weapon supply. Empty. He'd thrown his last knife at the enemy who'd been shooting at him.

He looked around, careful not to expose too much of his head. There! A sword was stuck into a wagon only a few feet away. Hendrix prepared to make a run for it.

And then the whole world went red.

He took off his headset and tossed it on the couch.

"Seriously, Kane?" he yelled. "How did

you get a laser blaster in ancient Japan?"

Hendrix's best friend appeared in the doorway connecting their hotel rooms. He had his headset around his neck and was twirling the cord in his hand.

"Transport bag," Kane said with an evil grin. "I bought it in Jupiter 3412. It just came out yesterday. I can take anything anywhere now."

"That's not fair!" Hendrix said. The whole point of *Time Hunters*, their favorite game, was that you had to make do with only the resources of the time and place the portal took you to. Everyone started each new mission with nothing. That made the game a lot harder—but it also kept the wallet warriors from buying up extras and taking over. That was the biggest thing Kane used to complain about when they used to play *Solar Surfers*.

And now he'd done exactly that himself.

"You cheated," Hendrix said.

Kane shrugged. "If the game allows it, it's not cheating. It's just good strategy."

Hendrix picked up his headset and slowly

twisted up the cord. He needed a moment to cool down. He couldn't afford to lose his temper. And he especially couldn't afford a fight with Kane right now. In less than nine hours they'd be starting a real-life mission— an episode for the show *Escape!*—with their friends Raymon and Ander.

Hendrix jumped at the sound of a knock on the door. Before he could ask who was there, Kane opened it. Ms. Pinkney, the show's production manager, stood there with her arms crossed. Despite the light pink suit and high heels, she reminded Hendrix of Ama Amanda, *Time Hunters'* most popular female avatar. Only Ms. Pinkney was twice as fierce.

"Lights out was almost an hour ago," she said.

"Like we're going to be able to sleep tonight anyway," Kane said. He crossed his own arms and stared right back at her. Sometimes Hendrix admired the way Kane didn't back down from adults. But he couldn't see how arguing with the show's manager was a good idea.

"We were just finishing up," Hendrix said quickly. "This was . . . a last-minute study session."

Ms. Pinkney's lips drew into a tight line, and Hendrix thought she was trying hard not to laugh. Or maybe yell. He couldn't tell.

"We're going to sleep now. Right Kane?" Hendrix said, looking at his friend.

Kane yanked off his headset, rolling his eyes. But he went into his room and shut the door without complaining. Hendrix sighed in relief.

Ms. Pinkney walked over and put a hand on Hendrix's shoulder. "I'm counting on you to be a good role model, Hendrix," she said. "I need to know that when you boys go in tomorrow, you'll make sure everyone stays on track."

Hendrix squirmed. Before they came to California, he had been an average guy. He hung out with his family, did well in school, and spent most of his free time playing video games with his friends. When Raymon had suggested they apply to be on *Escape!*, Hendrix had only agreed because he figured it wouldn't go anywhere.

So he'd made himself sound as good as possible when they'd filmed their audition tape. He said he was a natural leader who loved to help people achieve their goals. It was true he'd been voted the group leader in his church's youth group. And he really did volunteer at the youth center twice a week, working with the little kids there. But if he'd known they would actually be chosen to participate on the show, he would have kept his mouth shut.

When they each filmed their pre-show interview pieces yesterday, Ms. Pinkney kept asking Hendrix how he was planning to lead the team. Hendrix had no choice but to play along. So now he was stuck. He told the whole world that he would take charge, making sure everyone followed the rules and did their best. The clips from the interviews were going to be used as filler between scenes of them in the *Escape!* house when the show aired in a couple of weeks.

Of course, first he and his team actually had to make it out of the house. And if they didn't, it would be all his fault. Hendrix couldn't stand the thought of letting his friends down, especially now that he knew they would be counting on him more than ever.

"Don't forget, you're the leader of this group," Ms. Pinkney reminded him. As if he could forget. "Get some sleep. You've got a big day ahead of you tomorrow."

Kane was right. Hendrix was never going to be able to get to sleep now.

CHAPTER

2

"Stop doing that," Kane growled at the woman trying to pat him down with makeup. She'd been following him around for the last half hour.

"Let her do her job," Hendrix said. "We can't start until you're done."

Kane glared at Hendrix. Then he dropped into a chair and the woman went to work. Hendrix, Raymon, and Ander had been ready for ages. Ms. Pinkney had dressed them in brand-name jeans they couldn't afford and T-shirts advertising products they didn't use. Their hair had been combed into styles they didn't wear. And, of course, there was the makeup.

"You'll thank me later," the woman said to Kane as she finished. "The cameras are very unforgiving."

To be fair, the makeup wasn't noticeable. It wasn't like they had on lipstick and fake eyelashes or anything. It was mostly what the woman called foundation. And she'd been oddly excited for the challenge of putting it on four boys with such different skin colors.

"All right, gentlemen!" Ms. Pinkney rushed through the door as soon as Kane was on his feet, as if she'd been watching them. "Follow me—it's almost show time."

The boys followed Ms. Pinkney to the green room. They found breakfast laid out for them, but they were all too nervous to do more than pick at the food. Except Kane. He loaded a plate and started cramming food in his mouth.

"What?" he asked as the others stared at him. "This might be our last chance to fill up on food until we're out."

Hendrix thought he had a point, but before he could convince his stomach it needed the food, Ms. Pinkney motioned for him to join her in the hallway.

"Good luck in there, Hendrix. Remember that even though you're here to win, we also want you to have a good time. Be yourself and do your best. We're all expecting great things from you."

Hendrix was sure Ms. Pinkney meant to be reassuring, but her words made him twice as anxious. What if his best wasn't good enough? He was nervous enough about the competition. The fear of making a fool of himself on camera made it worse. But knowing that everyone expected him to be in charge was almost too much.

Ms. Pinkney spent a few moments talking to each of the other boys. Then she led them to the set where they would start filming.

"Before we go in, we need to go over the rules one last time," Ms. Pinkney said.

Hendrix could probably recite the rules in his sleep. They had twelve hours to solve the puzzles that would help them get out of the house. If they escaped in time, they'd each get a $50,000 scholarship to put toward college. If they got out sooner, they got bonus money. The quicker they escaped, the bigger the reward. There would also be bonus puzzles in the house. They'd get additional prizes for solving those too.

Escaping the house would be the easy part. The hard part was being filmed every single minute of the contest.

Inside the house, the boys would wear tiny microphones and there would be cameras everywhere. They would have to stop in front of specific cameras to give progress reports throughout the competition. The only place to get any privacy would be the bathroom, and even then they would have to remember to turn off their microphones.

"And above all else," Ms. Pinkney said when she got to the end of her speech, "give the viewers a good show!"

Hendrix swallowed hard. It wasn't enough to just play the game. They had to make it interesting for all the people watching. Ms. Pinkney had told Hendrix that was one of his most important jobs as the leader.

They lined up outside the door. Hendrix took a couple deep breaths to steady his racing heart. Ms. Pinkney gave him a nod, and he turned to his friends. "Okay, guys. Let's do this."

Hendrix opened the door, and the four boys stepped over the threshold and into darkness. They heard a soft click as the door locked behind them.

CHAPTER
3

Hendrix found a light switch and flipped it on.
The boys found themselves standing in an old
kitchen. It was decorated in hideous shades of
green and orange. Just like in *Time Hunters*—
the sponsor for this episode of *Escape!*—each
room would be from a different time and place.
Hendrix guessed this room was supposed to be
from the 1960s United States. The only thing
that didn't fit was the digital countdown clock
on the wall.

This is it, Hendrix thought. Ms. Pinkney
had told him that he had to make the first
move—make sure everyone knew he was

in charge from the very beginning. "Okay, everyone," Hendrix called. His voice wavered a little, so he swallowed and tried again. "Tell me what you see."

Everyone started talking at once. Hendrix tried to hear what they were saying, but couldn't make sense of any of it.

"Wait!" he yelled. To his surprise, the other three stopped talking and turned to him. Hendrix felt a flicker of hope. Maybe he could do this after all. "One at a time," he said. "Raymon, you first."

"The clock," Raymon said. He pointed to a large clock over the stove. "It's stopped at ten thirty-two. It might be a clue."

"Good. Anyone else?" Hendrix looked at Kane, who had been shouting something before Hendrix had called on Raymon. Kane crossed the kitchen to the only other door in the room. He tried the handle and shook his head. "It's locked—it looks like we'll need to find a regular key to unlock it."

Ander said, "I think we need to look through all the cabinets and drawers."

"Good ideas, everyone," Hendrix said. "Remember, anything might be a clue." The boys started searching and quickly found a box locked with a padlock, a cabinet door that needed a key to unlock it, a stack of magazines with some of the pages folded over, and a notebook and pen.

"Try 1-0-3-2 on the padlock," Raymon suggested.

Kane turned the dials and tugged. "No luck," he said.

"Anything in those magazines that might help?" Hendrix asked.

Ander shook his head. "Too many numbers for the padlock. But there are letters circled on the pages. That might be something."

"Let's write everything we find in the notebook," Raymon suggested.

While Ander did that, the others got back to searching. Hendrix noticed a framed, cross-stitched poem on the wall. It read:

welcome Home friends
who are Family too

Never fear loneliness
when Love abounds

The poem was so strange, Hendrix thought it had to be a clue, but he couldn't figure out what it meant. *Then again, it could also be one of those bonus puzzles,* he thought. *Or it could mean nothing at all.* They'd been warned that not everything they found would be useful. He wrote it down in the notebook just in case and kept searching.

"This is ridiculous!" Kane shouted. "How are we supposed to get out of this house if we can't even get out of the kitchen?"

They had already opened every drawer and cabinet and looked in all the pots and pans at least twice. Hendrix glanced at the countdown clock. They'd been in the kitchen for twenty minutes and hadn't made any progress at all. He was afraid Kane was right.

"Hendrix!" A voice suddenly crackled through hidden speakers. "Please go to the mirror and give a status update." They all froze and looked around.

Hendrix had been expecting this, but he didn't like being singled out first. *What am I supposed to say?* he wondered. *Am I not doing a good enough job?*

The mirror, which hung over the sink where a window would usually be, looked ordinary at first. Then Hendrix saw a faint red glow in the corner.

"Tell us what's going on. What are you thinking and feeling right now?" the voice asked. Hendrix looked back at his friends, who were staring at him. They quickly got back to work, but he was sure they would be listening to every word he said.

"So, uh . . . we're in the first room. It's a kitchen. We've found a few things but no key or anything that will unlock the first door." He stopped and took a breath. *Give them a good show*, he remembered. He was the leader. He had to sound confident even if he didn't feel it. "It's not looking so good right now, but I'm sure we're missing something obvious. Once we get into the next room, I bet all this other stuff we've found will make sense."

Hendrix scratched his head and tried to think of something else to say. In the mirror he saw Kane stretch up to his full height and run his hand over the top of the doorframe.

"You've got to be kidding!" Kane held up a key and grinned. "It was right there the whole time."

"Well, go on and try it," Hendrix said, forgetting all about the mirror. The room was dead silent as the boys held their breath while Kane slid the key into the lock.

Click.

The door swung open.

CHAPTER

4

"Yes!" Kane pumped his fist in the air and gave everyone a high five. Hendrix wanted to rush through the door and get started on the next room, but he reminded himself again that they needed to put on a good show. Even though it wasn't much of a victory, it was the first they'd had and they needed to play it up. "Great job, Kane!" he yelled.

Ander had joined in the celebration, but Raymon was staring at the doorframe, shaking his head in disbelief. Hendrix slapped him on the back and said, "Let's see what they've got for us next."

Raymon seemed to catch on and gave a half-hearted smile as he followed Hendrix into the darkened room. Ander entered last and flipped on the light. When he did, the boys gasped.

This room was a living room, but clearly from the future. Everything was made of metal and glass and full of sharp edges. The floor was a dull steel. The furniture was the same color as the floor but seemed to be made out of hard plastic that didn't look comfortable at all. What might have been a bookshelf in a present-day living room was full of weird-looking gadgets. Half of another wall was flat and shiny, like a turned-off screen.

Kane went straight over to the shiny wall and pushed a button. "This is what I'm talking about!" he shouted as the screen flashed to life. But no matter what Kane did, it only showed a series of colored lines.

The room had three doors—one off to the left of where they'd come in, one directly across from the door they'd just come through, and another next to the TV wall. Raymon went to the door on the left and pushed it open.

"Found the bathroom," he called.

Ander tried the door across from where they came in. "Locked," he said. "It needs a key."

"This one has a keypad," Kane reported from the door next to the TV. He tried 1-0-3-2, but the light flashed red.

"Okay, let's look around." Hendrix held up the notebook. "If you find anything, write it in here in case we need it later."

Kane, who had gone back to fiddling with the TV, shot Hendrix an irritated look. Hendrix ignored it and joined Ander, who was examining the gadgets. Most of them didn't turn on or do anything that the boys could see. But they did find a tablet that fired up. It asked for a code, though.

"Hey, Raymon," Ander called. "What was the time on the kitchen clock again?"

"Ten thirty-two."

Ander entered the numbers and the tablet opened to a game. Ander took it to the couch to work on it. Hendrix felt bad that he hadn't thought to try that. He was supposed to be in charge, but so far he hadn't solved a single thing.

"Raymon, please report to the kitchen for a status update," the voice called out.

Hendrix looked at the countdown clock in this room and was shocked to find they were almost a full hour in already. He went back to the gadgets, hoping to find a key or a code in one of them. He noticed one that seemed different from the rest. It was made of metal and had many twisted joints, but Hendrix couldn't get it to do anything useful.

"Find something?" Kane asked.

"I don't know," Hendrix said.

"I think it's a puzzle box." Kane took the object from Hendrix and started pushing and pulling. Hendrix was about to tell him to give it back when it popped open and a small key fell out.

Kane rushed over to try the key in the far door. "It's too small," he said.

"Maybe it goes to the cabinet in the kitchen," Raymon said, returning from his status check.

They all ran back to the kitchen and watched as Kane tried the key on the locked cabinet. This time the key was too big. It didn't even fit all the way in.

"That figures," Kane grumbled. He dropped the key on the floor and walked out of the room.

Ander picked it up and carefully tucked it into the notebook. "Now what?" he asked.

"I guess we keep looking," Raymon said as they headed back to the living room.

The problem was there weren't many places left to look. They'd gone over everything in the kitchen and living room already. *Wait,* Hendrix thought, *if the living room is supposed to be from the future, there might be hidden panels in the walls or voice-activated doors.*

He stopped and looked around. The wall next to the shelves of gadgets was sticking out farther than the other walls, making it even with the edge of the shelves. Maybe there were secret compartments in there. Feeling a little silly, Hendrix slid his hands all over the metal, stopping occasionally to tap gently. He could feel a nearly invisible seam, but he couldn't figure out how to open it.

He knew he should ask for help. Raymon could probably get it open with his eyes closed. But Hendrix felt he had to do something on his own to prove he was the leader, so he didn't say anything.

"Hey, guys! I think I've got something," Ander said, excited.

Hendrix joined Kane and Raymon as they gathered around Ander, who was holding up the tablet for them to see. The screen was filled with dots in different colors and sizes floating all over.

"I solved the game and it went to this," Ander said. "Any ideas?"

Something about the colors tugged at Hendrix. He asked for the tablet, which Ander handed over. There were a lot of reds, whites, purples, and greens, but not nearly as many in yellow, blue, orange, or gray—the same colors that were frozen on the TV screen. It was hard to keep track with the way everything was bumping around, but after a minute he was able to count the number of dots in each of those colors

"Seven, one, eight, two," Hendrix said. The others stared, but he kept repeating the numbers as he found the locked box from the kitchen and turned the dials of the padlock. When he got them all lined up he took a deep breath and tugged.

The padlock slid open.

Inside was a key.

"I bet this is for the door," Kane said.

Before Hendrix could say anything, Kane grabbed the key and bolted to the door on the far side of the room. By the time the others reached him, Kane had pushed the door open and was gazing openmouthed into a long hallway that stretched out on either side of the doorway.

Hendrix couldn't help feeling proud. *I actually solved something*, he thought. *I can do this.*

CHAPTER

5

The hallway looked as if it could have come from a medieval castle. The walls seemed to be rough stone. Hendrix ran his hand over one wall, expecting it to be wallpaper. He was surprised to find the stone was uneven and very real. Suits of armor stood guard next to two doors, one on either end of the hall. Other than that, the hallway was empty.

"I think we should try to get the other door in the living room open before we go on," Raymon said.

Kane, who was already halfway to the door on the right, stopped and turned around.

"Why? There might not even be anything in there. I say we push forward."

"But what if we're supposed to do things in a certain order?" Raymon asked. "We could waste a lot of time if we've missed something."

"You think you're so much smarter than the rest of us, don't you, Raymon?" Kane said. He clenched his fists and took a step toward him.

"Hey!" Hendrix rushed to stand between the two. His heart was pounding. If Kane and Raymon got into a fight, it could ruin everything. They still had eleven hours to go, so they had to get along.

"We're doing really well so far because we're working together. We're a team. Let's not start fighting now." He looked from Kane to Raymon, then over at Ander, making eye contact with each of his friends. "Raymon might be right," he said, holding up a hand as Kane tried to interrupt. "But I don't see the harm in seeing what's next, either. Chances are those doors are locked anyway, right?"

Raymon nodded in agreement, but Kane just crossed his arms and glared.

"So why don't we check?" Ander suggested.

Hendrix nodded and Ander took off toward the door at the left end of the hallway while Kane continued to the other one.

"This one's locked," Ander said. "It needs a key."

"Mine's unlocked," Kane called, sounding a little smug. He opened the door and disappeared for a moment before popping his head back through. "There's stairs."

By the time Hendrix got to the door, Kane was already halfway up the steps. There was another set of stairs that led down.

"I'll go down and check," Ander said.

A moment later both boys were back to report the doors at the ends of the stairs were locked and had keypads.

"Okay," Hendrix said. "So we need three codes. One for each of the doors in the stairwell and one for the last door in the living room. And we need a key for the other door in the hallway. We're still a step closer than we were before. At least now we know what we need."

"Yeah, right." Kane bumped Hendrix's shoulder hard as he brushed past.

"Kane," Hendrix called after him. But then he stopped. He couldn't just be Kane's friend now. He had to look out for the whole team. Luckily, the voice called Kane for a status update as soon as they got back to the living room.

Hendrix went back to the shelf with the gadgets, but he couldn't take his eyes off the wall next to it. He was sure there was something there, but he still didn't know how to open it. He decided to take all of the gadgets to the coffee table by the couch and spread them out.

"What are you doing?" Ander asked.

"I'm not sure," Hendrix said. He immediately regretted the words and looked around anxiously for the hidden cameras watching his every move. "I mean, I'm not sure yet. But I was thinking maybe we need to see all of these together. They might be a puzzle or something."

Ander rubbed the back of his head and gave Hendrix an odd look. But then he shrugged and started checking the things out all over again.

Hendrix didn't know Ander as well as he knew Kane and Raymon. Ander had only moved to their town three years ago, at the beginning of eighth grade. At first, Hendrix thought Ander was one of the popular, snobby kids. He played football and baseball and always wore fashionable, expensive clothes. But he never really seemed to fit in with the popular crowd. Still, Hendrix had been surprised when Raymon mentioned that Ander played *Time Hunters* and wanted to join their league.

Raymon was pretty surprising that way too. He was a nerd. There was no other word for it, and no need for one since that's what Raymon called himself. Straight As in all the hardest classes, on student council since fifth grade, chess club, math club. . . . If you could think of something geeky, Raymon was in it. He also loved video games. And once Hendrix got to know him, he found out Raymon was really funny.

Kane had never really warmed up to Raymon, though. And since Ander was more Raymon's friend than Hendrix's, Kane was even less close to him. Hendrix might not feel like much of a leader right now, but he definitely felt like the glue that held this group together.

Suddenly, an angry voice interrupted Hendrix's thoughts.

"Have you just been sitting here the whole time?" Kane demanded, glaring at Raymon as he rejoined the group.

"I'm thinking," Raymon said, his voice defensive. "We've looked everywhere and found lots of clues. Now we just have to figure them out."

"Well, I don't think staring off into space is helping much. You need to pull your weight," Kane snapped.

Raymon opened his mouth to protest but closed it again.

"You know, I have to agree with Kane . . ." Ander said. He bit his lip and didn't say anything else.

Hendrix felt like he should say something

to calm everyone down. But he had no idea what to do. He agreed with Kane that they needed to keep looking. But he could see Raymon's point too. And all he and Ander were really doing with these gadgets was trying to make it look like they were doing something. But they were getting nowhere.

Still, it was his job to keep everyone on track and working together. He stood up.

"Let's all calm down. We're only . . ." He looked at the clock and swallowed hard. "We're less than two hours in and we've opened three doors already."

"But we don't know how many rooms there are," Ander pointed out.

Hendrix nodded. "That's true. But all we can do is take it one step at a time. Kane, what do you think we should do right now?"

Kane blinked, like he wasn't expecting Hendrix to ask his advice. "I . . . I think we need to keep looking," he said. "All of us," he added with a glare at Raymon.

"Okay. Let's go back over every inch of these two rooms and see if there's anything we missed. Raymon, Ander, why don't you two go back to the kitchen, and Kane and I will work in here. If neither of us has found anything in fifteen minutes, we'll switch."

"Sounds like a plan," Ander said.

Hendrix looked at Raymon, who mumbled something and followed Ander back to the kitchen.

Kane glared at Hendrix and said, "Whatever you say." Then, after he'd turned his back, he added, "Boss."

CHAPTER

6

Another half hour had passed and they were
no closer to getting any of the doors open.
They'd found a couple more potential clues,
but nothing that would open a door. Hendrix
started to wonder if this whole show was a
big sham. Maybe there was no way through
the rest of the doors and this was some kind
of psychological experiment to see how much
he and his friends could stand before they
self-destructed.

If so, they were pretty close.

"This is ridiculous. Maybe we should just
call it quits and save ourselves the humiliation,"

Kane said, as if he were reading Hendrix's thoughts.

"There's got to be something we're missing," Hendrix said, even though he didn't really believe it himself anymore.

"I was thinking . . ." Ander said. They all looked at him but he didn't go on.

"Well, gee. Thanks for that profound announcement," Kane said, rolling his eyes.

Hendrix felt the corners of his mouth twitch. Kane was being a jerk, and it wasn't even that funny, but for some reason he felt like laughing. It must be the stress.

"What were you thinking?" Hendrix asked when he was sure he was under control.

"It was your idea, really," Ander said. "You said we should look at all the gadgets at once to see if they went together somehow."

"Which they didn't," Kane said.

Hendrix ignored him and motioned for Ander to go on.

"What if that's true for all the clues we've found? Like, the time on the clock was the password for the tablet. And then the tablet and the TV were a set that helped open the lock box."

"In case you haven't noticed, we've already been trying things together," Kane said.

"No, Ander's right," Raymon said. It was the first time Hendrix had heard him speak since his clash with Kane. "Not just solving one thing and using it to solve another. I think we need to combine the clues."

Raymon jumped up, his face suddenly more excited and hopeful than Hendrix had seen since he found the ad about being a contestant on *Escape!* He grabbed the notebook and started tearing out pages.

"Hey!" Kane yelled furiously, but Raymon just ignored him.

"Yes! Look at this. The poem from the kitchen that Hendrix found. It doesn't mean anything by itself. But what if we match up the capitalized letters from the poem with the letters circled on the pages of the magazines from the kitchen? I bet those page numbers make a four-digit code."

He laid two pieces of paper side by side and

the other boys gathered around to look. One was the poem, the other a list of page numbers and the letters that had been circled on each. Like with the tablet and the TV, there were many more than they needed to make a code. Some of the letters repeated several times and some of the page numbers were double digits.

But H, F, N, and L only had one match apiece—and only with single digit page numbers.

Raymon wrote the resulting code on a piece of paper. Kane reached for it, but Raymon swatted his hand away. They all stared at Raymon in disbelief.

"There's more. Look," Raymon said.

The others watched as he pulled more pages out of the notebook and put them together. Hendrix was surprised to see clues he didn't even know the others had gathered. It made him feel a little better about not sharing his suspicion about the possible hidden door in the wall.

In the end, Raymon came up with another four-digit code plus a six-digit code. The doors at the top and bottom of the stairs and the other door in the living room all had keypads, so these had to be for those. He copied down all three codes on three pieces of paper.

"All right," Hendrix said as soon as Raymon finished. "Let's go try these."

"I'll take the upstairs," Kane said. He grabbed one of the pieces of paper out of Raymon's hand and rushed off.

"If you get in, come back down and let us know!" Hendrix shouted, but his friend never even looked back. "I'll check the downstairs," he said. "You guys check out the one in this room, and we'll all meet back here."

Despite his irritation with Kane, Hendrix was eager to try out the codes. He was sure they were finally getting somewhere.

But none of the codes worked on the door at the bottom of the stairs. He tried them forward and backward and in every possible combination, but the keypad flashed red no matter what he did.

Hoping his friends had better luck, he trudged back up the stairs and to the living room. Ander and Raymon were waiting with a hopeful look, but the living room door was still firmly closed. Hendrix just shook his head.

"Did you try—"

"I tried everything," Hendrix said, cutting Raymon off. Didn't he have any faith in Hendrix at all? "Where's Kane?"

"He didn't come back down," Ander said. "We thought he was with you."

The three boys stared at each other for a moment, then all took off running. The door at the top of the stairs was open. They rushed through and found themselves in a room that looked like the deck of a spaceship.

"Is this for real?" Ander asked.

The room was round, and the far side of it was covered with monitors showing outer space. Four large chairs faced the screens. On both sides of the room were rows of floor-to-ceiling cabinets, and there was a table in the center of the room.

"This is the flight deck of the O.S.G. *Trangoloper!*" Raymon shrieked. "It looks exactly the same as in the game."

"Oh, it's better than that," Kane said, popping out from behind one of the cabinets. "It's also a fully stocked kitchen!" Kane grinned, a bag of chips and can of soda clutched in his hands.

CHAPTER

7

"We really should get back to looking for clues," Hendrix said thirty minutes, one sandwich, and two cans of soda later. But he made no move to get up from the surprisingly comfortable flight chair where he'd been zoning out, watching the stars glide by. The others nodded, but no one looked like they were in much of a hurry to get back to work.

To be fair, they'd done a pretty good job searching the fridge and cabinets where the food was stored. Unfortunately, there didn't seem to be any clues hiding in the chips and cookies.

Hendrix knew it had to be up to him to the get the others motivated, no matter how much he was also enjoying this little break. He got to his feet and started looking through the cabinets on the other side of the room.

After a few moments, Ander and Raymon joined him. Raymon examined the monitors. As he ran his hand around the edge of one, the screen switched from the image of deep space to a rectangle with lines across it and x's at various points all over.

"I think that's a football field," Ander said. "And these x's could be yard lines. But I'm not sure why they're all over or what the order should be."

Realizing they hadn't brought the notebook with them, Ander went to grab it. As soon as he left, Raymon found an old-fashioned, 500-piece puzzle in one of the cabinets.

"This is weird," Raymon said. "It seems out of place. Everything else is so high-tech, but this is just an ordinary puzzle."

"Not to mention you couldn't really do a puzzle in zero gravity," Hendrix pointed out.

"That must mean it's a clue." Raymon took the puzzle to the table and dumped the pieces out.

"Or it could mean nothing at all," Kane said. "Seems like a pretty good way to get people to waste a bunch of time when they should be working."

"As if you're working so hard," Hendrix retorted. "You're still sitting there while we're searching this place top to bottom." Kane was his best friend, but he was getting more and more irritated with him the longer they were in this house.

"I deserve a break!" Kane burst out. "I've done more than the rest of you. And I'm not the one who wants to waste his time putting together some stupid puzzle."

"How have you—" Hendrix started at the same time that Raymon said, "It's not stupid if it's a clue!" Pretty soon, all three of the boys were yelling so much that Hendrix had lost track of what they were even arguing about.

"Whoa!" Ander's voice cut through and

the others fell silent. "I was gone for like two minutes. What happened?"

Hendrix's cheeks burned when he realized how foolish he'd been acting. And also that Ander was acting like more of a leader than he was. Raymon also seemed to realize he'd gotten out of control, and he sat down and let his head fall into his hands. Kane was the only one who didn't calm down. He pushed past Ander and went down the stairs without a word.

"Maybe we should each work on our own for a little while," Ander suggested. "I think we could all use some time to ourselves."

"Ander," the voice boomed. "Please report for a status update."

Hendrix felt his blood run cold. Ander was doing *his* job, and he was much better at it than Hendrix had been. The producers were probably going to tell Ander he was in charge now. Maybe that was for the best.

He looked up to try to catch Ander's attention, to let him know it was okay. But Ander looked utterly terrified, like he was the one who had screwed up instead of Hendrix.

He stood frozen for a moment, then practically ran out the door.

Hendrix turned to Raymon, who had looked up when the voice called Ander. He looked as surprised and upset as Hendrix felt.

"It isn't supposed to be like this," he said.

"What do you mean?" Hendrix asked.

Raymon's head jerked, like he'd forgotten that Hendrix was there when he spoke. "Nothing. I just mean . . . I didn't think it would be this hard."

"I don't think we're doing that bad," Hendrix said. He secretly agreed with Raymon but knew he had to at least sound confident. "It's only been three hours and we've gotten pretty far."

Raymon shook his head. "I don't mean the show. I mean us. We've never fought before, except when we were gaming. It never spilled over into real life."

"Well, this isn't really real life, is it?" Hendrix said. "It is a game. And win or lose, in a day or two we'll be back home, getting ready to start our junior year, and life will be as boring as it ever was." He tried to sound reassuring, but Hendrix couldn't help thinking that Raymon had a point.

Raymon looked at him, eyes wide behind his glasses. "I hope you're right."

Hendrix felt a pang of concern run through him as he remembered the dirty looks Kane gave him, the way he called him "boss," how he kept walking away instead of trying to talk things out. Kane had been his best friend since first grade. And his friendship was worth more to Hendrix than any scholarship or prize money. He hoped Kane felt the same.

"I'm going back downstairs," Hendrix said. "You go ahead and get working on that puzzle."

"So do you think it's a clue?" Raymon asked eagerly.

"I'm not sure about anything right now," Hendrix admitted as he left the room.

Ander was still in the kitchen giving his status update when Hendrix got downstairs. Kane was on the couch poking at the gadgets, but he didn't seem to be making much of an effort. Hendrix wanted to work on the wall panel again, but more than anything he wanted to be alone. The only other place to go was the hallway, so that was where he went.

CHAPTER

8

Hendrix stared at the countdown clock, which showed a little over seven hours. They'd been in the house nearly six hours already. He did the math in his head and figured it was probably early afternoon in the real world. There was no other way to tell—the countdown clock was the only thing keeping track of time, there were no windows in the house, and his stomach was so twisted in knots that he couldn't trust it to let him know how long it had been since the snack in the flight deck room.

Of course, he could probably count the fights he and his friends had gotten into as a way of measuring their time in the *Escape!* house. If so, time was going faster and faster the longer they were in there. He'd hoped it would slow down when they'd split up a while ago. Hendrix had spent close to an hour in the medieval hallway searching the suits of armor, the walls, the staircases, even the floors. He'd found some markings on the armor and a pattern to the cracks in the floor, but he doubted they were important.

The others hadn't had much more luck. Raymon had spent some time putting the puzzle together, but when he came back down to the living room, he told Hendrix he was halfway done and couldn't see anything that looked like a clue yet. Ander had gone over the kitchen and living room again. Like Hendrix, he had found a few more things that might have been clues or just random patterns. As far as Hendrix could tell, Kane had fallen asleep on the couch and had only woken up when he and Raymon came in.

For a half hour or so after they were all back together, they talked about what they had, what they thought they still needed to find or do, and what kinds of puzzles might still be waiting for them. Their discussion encouraged them to get back to searching, but before long they were back to either fighting or ignoring each other. Even the producers must have been getting bored because they were calling the boys to the mirror for status updates more often.

"Which college do you plan to attend if you win the scholarship?" the voice asked Hendrix as he was giving his fourth status update so far.

"I want to go to West Point, join the military, and make my family proud." He'd seen enough other reality TV shows to know that was the kind of answer they liked.

"Tell us about your family."

Hendrix rubbed the back of his neck and looked away from the mirror. They'd already asked him this during the interview before they started filming. He'd barely been able to keep himself from crying then. They must have known that now—tired and upset from all the fighting—he'd break down completely.

That was what they wanted. A good show.

"It's me, my dad and stepmom, my brother, and my baby sister." When the voice didn't ask anything more, he knew he was expected to continue. *Maybe if I give them what they want, some clue will appear out of thin air,* he thought in irritation. He wouldn't be surprised if the show was rigged that way. Hendrix took a long breath in and held it. He let the next sentence come out as quickly as possible. "My mom died when I was ten."

There. He'd said it. But the voice remained silent, and even though no one was demanding he talk, Hendrix felt like he had to explain. He had to tell everyone how wonderful she was and how much it sucked that she was gone.

"My parents met in the army. Mom had planned to stay in the army for her full career. My dad was only going to serve four years and then go to college. But when they fell in love, they both decided to get out. Dad went into the reserves, but Mom decided she wanted to start a family and thought it wouldn't be safe to have both parents still in the military."

Hendrix gave a bitter laugh. "I guess you can take the woman out of the army, but you can't take the army out of the woman. She never stopped being a soldier. Never stopped wanting to help people. So when Mom saw a house on fire on her way home from the grocery store, she called 9-1-1 like any good person would. But when she heard a baby crying inside, she ran in to rescue him. There were other people there, just standing around. But my mom is the one who went in and saved that baby."

Hendrix could see the tears pooling in his eyes in the mirror, but aside from that, his face didn't show any sign of the pain welling up inside him. Pain, and a little bit of anger. Anger at the people who didn't help and who didn't try to stop his mom from risking her life. At the people who fell asleep smoking, putting themselves and their baby in so much danger. At his mom, for saving that baby instead of herself.

"She was badly burned," Hendrix continued, wiping his eyes. "The doctors did everything they could, but she died two days later." Hendrix turned away from the mirror until he was able to get control of himself. There was so much more he could say about his mother. In fact, he could spend the rest of the seven hours they had left remembering her.

He could spend the rest of his life thinking about everything he'd lost that day.

But what good would that do? he thought, looking at his face in the mirror. *I need to try to move on with my life. And getting a college scholarship is a good way to start.*

Hendrix left the kitchen without waiting to be dismissed.

CHAPTER

9

"I think I've got another code." Raymon's voice
was subdued, considering they were more than
five hours in and it was the first breakthrough
they'd had in a long time. Or maybe it had
something to do with the fact that Ander had
just handed Raymon the code and explained
it to him. At least, that's the way it looked to
Hendrix. Something about that bothered him,
but he was too eager to try out this new code
to worry just now.

"Let's try it," Kane said. He was on his feet
and about to snatch the paper out of Raymon's
hand—the way he'd been doing this whole

game—but Hendrix was closer and quicker.

"We need to make another copy and try it on both of the remaining doors with keypads. We still have the one at the bottom of the stairs, remember?" he said as he took the paper from Raymon. *I want to be the one to open a door for once, Kane,* Hendrix thought bitterly.

"Yeah, and I also remember that this door is right here and will take all of ten seconds to try before we go to the other one. So why waste time copying it down?" Kane said, getting right up in Hendrix's face.

"Why waste time arguing about it at all?" Ander asked. While Hendrix and Kane were fighting with each other, Ander went over to the door and started entering the code. They both turned as he put in the last number and the light turned green.

It had been two hours since they'd gotten into the flight deck upstairs. Hendrix was so used to disappointment at this point that it took a second for his brain to realize what green meant. The others must have been feeling the same because no one moved for the space of several excited heartbeats. Then the moment passed and they all rushed forward at once, practically running Ander over in the process.

After the flight deck, Hendrix was expecting something amazing. But this room was . . . boring. It looked like an ordinary, living room—smaller than the futuristic room, more like a den. It had a love seat facing a TV and a small table with two chairs. Other than the entertainment center and a fireplace, every inch of the walls was covered in bookshelves. And unlike in the futuristic living room, these bookshelves were packed with real books. Raymon was already taking them down and looking through the pages. *At least there are no new doors in here*, Hendrix thought.

Kane, naturally, had gone straight to the TV. This one clicked on to a commercial, but when Kane tried to change the channel it only alternated between the commercial and the input screen. It didn't take long for Kane to get frustrated and turn it off.

"Not even a clue this time," he growled.

"Maybe that commercial means something," Raymon suggested.

Hendrix thought he might be right. It didn't seem like a real TV ad. But he was more interested in the input screen.

"Is there a DVD player or something?" he asked.

Kane pulled on the cabinet doors below the TV but they were locked.

"Where's that key Kane found in the puzzle box?" Hendrix asked.

"We tried it in the living room door and then the kitchen cabinet," Raymon remembered.

"I put it in the notebook," Ander said. He found the key and tossed it to Kane, who tried it in the lock. This time it fit perfectly. Hendrix heard the lock click open and Kane opened the doors.

"Holy . . ." Kane clapped a hand over his mouth, obviously remembering the show's prohibition on swearing. "Look at this, guys."

"What?" Hendrix asked, alarmed at the look on Kane's face. He seemed to be on the verge of tears. "What is it?"

Kane swung the cabinet doors open so the rest of them could see.

"It's a SquarePot NG," he whispered.

The collective gasp from the other three boys was the only sound in the room for several long seconds after Kane's announcement. The SquarePot was their gaming system of choice, but they all had the original version. None of them had been able to convince their parents to buy the SquarePot Q when it came out last year. The Next Generation version wasn't due to hit stores until next month.

"And look," Kane said, grinning and holding up a video game case.

"Oh, we have to play that," Ander declared.

Hendrix was very glad Ander was the one to suggest it. If it had been Kane, the others might have argued. As the leader, Hendrix felt he should insist they get to work searching this room for clues. But he was sure even Raymon wanted to try out the latest version of *Time Hunters*, which also wouldn't be released until next month.

"They said there were would be bonus puzzles," Hendrix said, hoping to mask his own desire to check out the game. "I bet this is one of them."

That was enough for the others, as if they'd needed any convincing. They settled in and played for about an hour, exploring all the new worlds, past and future. As he had discovered in the online version, though, there were updates Hendrix didn't really care for. Players could purchase upgrades, transport weapons and gear across portals, and even choose which time and place they went to next if they did well enough in their current mission.

Hendrix didn't like it. And he was more than ready to quit when Raymon quietly suggested they get back to work. Ander also seemed glad for the excuse to stop. But Kane was loving the new version, taking advantage of the updates, finding cheats, and buying everything that was available with a seemingly unlimited spending account.

"Just a few more levels," he whined when the others signed out at the end of their current mission, in which Kane had, once again, kicked their butts all over the screen.

"I agree with Raymon. We probably should get back to it," Hendrix said. "We've only got six and a half hours left. And there's bound to be tons of clues in here."

"I thought you were my best friend," Kane said quietly. Hendrix couldn't decide if he sounded more angry or hurt. But Kane was right. They were best friends. Maybe if Hendrix showed Kane that was still true, he'd start acting more like a member of the team.

"Okay. Two more levels," he agreed. He shot an apologetic look at Ander and Raymon, who shook their heads and left the room.

Kane grinned and started the game back up for just the two of them. But two levels turned into three, and then four. When Kane started the fifth, Hendrix decided he'd had enough.

"What are you doing?" Kane asked as Hendrix's half of the screen went black.

"I'm getting back to work."

"Okay," Kane agreed, surprising Hendrix by not arguing. He hoped his plan had worked—that Kane had dropped the attitude. But then Kane added, "Bring me down a sandwich, would you? I'm starving."

And Hendrix realized nothing had changed.

CHAPTER 10

The countdown clock hit exactly 6:00. They were six hours in and had six hours to go. Hendrix was sure they were close to the end, but they would never get there if they couldn't move forward. And to do that, they needed to search the den.

After Hendrix had left Kane, he'd found Ander and Raymon in the flight deck room. Raymon was back at work on the puzzle. Ander was methodically searching for anything they might have missed. They'd looked so hopeful when Hendrix walked in, like they expected him to say he'd solved a clue. Or at least gotten Kane to quit playing. He'd felt so guilty about his failure as a leader that he'd stayed downstairs after delivering Kane's food.

At some point, Kane will have to take a break from the game, Hendrix thought desperately. *Or he'll get called for a status update or take an extra-long bathroom break. Something.* Maybe he was being a coward, but Hendrix's plan was to wait for Kane to leave on his own and then go search the den.

"Hendrix, we've got a problem," Ander said as he came into the kitchen. Raymon was right behind him, nodding his agreement.

"I know," Hendrix said. "We need to search the den."

"It's more than that," Raymon said. "It's the fact that we're all too afraid to go in there while Kane's playing. We're afraid of *him*."

"I'm not—" Hendrix stopped, realizing Raymon was right. Kane was being a bully. He might not be outright threatening anyone, but his bad attitude was keeping them from being a team. Hendrix was Kane's friend. But he was also the leader of this team—and he owed it to Ander and Raymon to stand up to Kane.

"All right," Hendrix said. "Let's go."

The others stayed a few steps behind him as he marched into the den and right up next to the TV so Kane would have to see him.

"We need to talk," Hendrix said in what he hoped was a firm and confident voice. Kane barely looked up. "We're halfway through and we have no idea how much farther we have to go. It's time to get back to work, and it's time we all did it together."

"In a few minutes," Kane said. "Just let me finish this level."

Something snapped in Hendrix. He turned and ripped the TV cord from the wall. The screen went blank and the room was filled with a sudden silence.

"What the—?" Kane jumped to his feet and took a step forward, but Hendrix refused to back down.

"Do I have your attention now?" Hendrix yelled angrily.

"Why are you being such a jerk?"

This only made Hendrix angrier. "Me? I'm the one being a jerk? You're the one sitting here doing nothing but playing *Time Hunters*."

"I'm doing plenty. You let Raymon work on that stupid puzzle for hours. How is this any different?" Kane fell back onto the chair. "And why do you get to tell everyone what to do anyway?"

"I'm not telling you what to do," Hendrix said. "I'm asking you to be a part of this team. I'm asking you to help us win."

Kane laughed. "Like we have a chance. I mean, come on. We're a bunch of teenagers. We might as well enjoy the perks of being on this show while we can. Because tomorrow we're going home empty-handed."

Kane looked at Ander and Raymon, who were staring openmouthed and wide-eyed after his speech. "You know that, right?" he said.

To Hendrix's horror, he saw Ander nod slightly.

"So quit," Hendrix said. His words were so quiet he could barely hear them himself. But Kane must have heard because he was back on his feet and in Hendrix's face.

"Fine, I'll quit," he said. "But like you said, we're a team. So if I go, we all go. That's what being a team means, right?"

Hendrix swallowed hard and took a step backward. "No. It means we work together toward a common goal. And *I* want to win. Raymon, do you want to win?"

Raymon made a strangled kind of sound. Then he cleared his throat and said, "Yes," in a small voice.

"Do you, Ander?" Hendrix asked.

Despite his earlier resigned nod, Ander responded with an enthusiastic "Heck yeah!"

Hendrix turned back to Kane. "Our team is the people who want to win this—who believe we *can* win this. And this team is going to search this room, find clues, and get through the rest of the doors and whatever's waiting for us beyond them. So you can either help or get out of the way."

Hendrix turned to the nearest shelf and started looking through books. After a moment he saw Ander and Raymon doing the same

thing. He tried really hard not to look to see
if Kane was joining, but eventually he couldn't
stand it anymore and took a quick peek.

Kane was on his knees inspecting
the fireplace.

Hendrix let out a breath he didn't know he'd
been holding. Suddenly, he needed to be alone.
He went to the bathroom, hoping to have a
few minutes to himself with no one watching.
A few minutes when he didn't have to solve all
the problems. But as soon as he turned off his
microphone, someone knocked on the door.

With a heavy sigh, Hendrix opened the
door. Raymon stood there, looking nervous.
Without waiting for Hendrix to say anything,
he stepped inside, closed the door, and turned
off his own microphone.

"Did you read the contract?" Raymon
asked. Hendrix shook his head. He didn't think
even his parents had read it, but he wasn't
surprised that Raymon had.

"Any player who does not complete the
competition is liable for all expenses incurred
by that player," Raymon said. He must have

seen that Hendrix wasn't following because he went on, "If we quit, we have to pay the studio back for everything they've given us. Airplane tickets, hotel rooms, food . . . who knows what else. But it would be a lot."

Hendrix gaped at him. "We can't let Kane quit then. We have to tell him."

Raymon shook his head. "He knows. I overheard him and one of the producers talking when I came out of my interview the other day. They stopped as soon as they saw me, but I know that's what they were talking about. So he definitely knows, and yet he's suggesting we all quit."

Hendrix felt his blood run cold. Kane wasn't just being lazy and unhelpful.

Kane was trying to sabotage them.

CHAPTER 11

It didn't take long to search the den once they were all working together. Hendrix had been wrong about the books all being real. It turned out the books on the top and bottom shelves were fake. They went through at least a hundred of the real books, but only two had anything that looked like clues. One had page numbers and letters circled, like in the magazines. In the other they found strange symbols, almost like hieroglyphs, written in the margins.

Kane discovered the same kind of markings etched into the stone of the fireplace. Ander realized the commercial kept repeating the phrase "green apples bear fruit." That was it. They had four new clues. Now they just needed to make sense of them.

It didn't take long for Kane to give up and go back to playing *Time Hunters*. That didn't surprise Hendrix, but he was disappointed when Raymon also stopped searching to go work on the puzzle again. Now Hendrix and Ander were alone in the living room, trying to figure out how to turn the clues they'd found into working codes.

Hendrix's eyes were starting to hurt as he studied the symbols they found in one of the books. "Any idea what these might be?" he asked.

Ander took the sheet Hendrix had been studying and shook his head. "If they mean anything at all we'd need a key to decode it. Maybe if we used the page numbers from the book where we found these we could . . ."

His voice trailed off. Hendrix thought at first it was because he was on to something, that he'd figured it out. But Ander put the paper down and bit his lip.

"What?" Hendrix asked.

"Nothing. I don't know. We should have Raymon work on it," Ander said, hesitating a bit.

"You don't think we're smart enough to figure it out on our own?" Hendrix asked.

"I'm not saying *you're* not smart," Ander said quickly. "Never mind. Let's just keep working."

Something felt very wrong to Hendrix. But he wasn't sure what it was, so there wasn't anything he could do about it.

"You know, I'm surprised we don't hang out more," Hendrix said, trying to change the subject. Sometimes when he stopped trying to solve a problem the answer came to him. And he had plenty of problems he couldn't solve right now.

"We do hang out," Ander said.

"Yeah, when we're playing *Time Hunters* online," said Hendrix. "But not so much in real life. I only just met your parents for the first time when we signed up for this show."

"I guess we don't have much in common," Ander said, not even looking up from the notes he was making.

Hendrix was surprised how much it hurt to hear Ander say that. "Well, yeah. I don't play sports like you, but that doesn't seem to keep you from being friends with Raymon."

Ander finally looked up, his forehead wrinkled and his lips pressed together. "I'm into more than just sports, you know. I'm a writer for the school newspaper, and I'm in the math club and on the debate team."

"Oh," Hendrix said, staring in surprise. He'd had no idea Ander was so involved. Or so smart. At school people in sports were easy to recognize because they wore their jerseys on game days. Everyone else just kind of blended in. There were no banners for kids who did theater or were on the honor roll. Since Hendrix knew Ander as a jock, it had never occurred to him he might be anything else.

"Is that how you met Raymon? Math club?" Hendrix asked.

"Yeah," Ander said. "How about you?"

"We were . . ." Hendrix trailed off. This was something he hadn't mentioned to anyone on the show. It wasn't that he was embarrassed.

In fact, it was more that it meant too much to him. "We were in orchestra together when we were younger."

Ander dropped his pen and stared at Hendrix in surprise. "You were in orchestra?"

"Why is that so shocking?" he challenged. Ander shrugged and tried to look less amazed. "I started playing violin when I was four, then switched to viola when I got bigger."

"Why'd you quit?" Ander asked, looking genuinely interested.

"My mom." Hendrix cleared his throat. "My mom was the one who loved music. When she died, it just got too hard. The music reminded me of her too much."

Hendrix hadn't planned to admit to Ander how much it had hurt to give up music. Or how much he missed his mom. But now that it was all out there, he felt relieved. Until he remembered it wasn't only Ander he'd just confessed his feelings to.

Trying hard not to look around for the cameras, Hendrix hurried to change the subject. "I'm sorry I never took the time to get to know you better before. I shouldn't have assumed you were just a dumb jock."

Ander flinched a little but then held out his hand. "I'm sorry too. I thought you and Kane were just slackers who played video games all day." Then he added, "I'm really glad we're doing this together."

Hendrix shook his hand. "Yeah. We make a pretty good team." Then he sighed, thinking about Kane. "You know, Kane isn't usually like this. He's actually one of the nicest people I know. He's the only person I ever felt I could be myself around. The only person who never judged me."

Ander's lip twitched slightly. "Even when you played the viola?"

Hendrix was about to give him a playful punch on the shoulder but stopped short when an idea popped into his head.

"Hey, where's that clue you found on the monitor upstairs? The one with the football field on it?"

Ander found it in the notebook and handed it over. Hendrix looked at it for a minute, then dug up one of the new clues they'd found in the den.

"I think these are music notes," he said.

"I'm pretty sure it's a football field," Ander said.

"No. I mean, yes, it is from side to side. But up and down, where these x's are." He drew lines across the page. "Sheet music has five lines like this. And the letters we found in the book in the den are only A through G, just like music notes."

Hendrix wrote the letters in, and then Ander matched them up with the numbers for the yard lines.

"Still too many numbers to be a code. But it's got to mean something," Ander said. "Let's go check with Raymon."

When they got upstairs they found Raymon asleep, his head resting on the now completed puzzle. Hendrix touched his arm and Raymon jumped to his feet, startled. He blinked, confused for a minute. Then he looked at Hendrix and Ander like he was about to cry.

"Don't tell Kane," he said before they had a chance to say anything about their clue.

"Don't tell Kane what?" Ander asked.

"The puzzle. He was right. It's not a clue. Just a stupid puzzle that I wasted my time on."

"Yeah, well, I doubt he's opening any doors playing *Time Hunters*," Hendrix said. "Don't worry. Besides, we found something."

He showed Raymon the clue and their solution. Raymon agreed they were on to something, but he wasn't sure what it meant either.

"I think we need to look at everything together again," Raymon said.

Hendrix agreed, but about more than just the clues. It had taken Ander's knowledge of football and his knowledge of music to put this clue together. *We're all going to have to work together if we want to succeed*, he thought. *That means Kane too.*

"Let's go get Kane and make a plan," he said. The others looked surprised, but for the first time since they entered the house, Hendrix was sure he was making the right call.

He walked out and the others followed. He was on the third step down when Raymon yelled out in excitement, "Guys! Look at this!"

Hendrix and Ander jogged back up quickly to find Raymon in the now mostly-dark room staring at the puzzle, which was glowing softly.

"I turned the light off on my way out. Habit, I guess. And when the lights went out a black light came on." He looked up with the first genuine smile Hendrix had seen since the cameras started rolling. "This puzzle is going to change everything!"

CHAPTER 12

"I don't see why you're so excited," Kane said when they told him what Raymon found on the puzzle. He shook his head and went back to playing *Time Hunters*.

"This is the biggest breakthrough we've had so far," Raymon insisted.

"It's just a clue, like all the others," Kane said. "It's going to lead to some other riddle that you'll get super jazzed about. And that will lead to another. It's a never-ending cycle. Don't you get it? There's no way to actually win. There's no point in even trying."

Hendrix opened his mouth, ready to ask

Kane why he was so convinced they were going to lose—or worse, quit and have to pay the studio back all that money. But he realized this wasn't the time or place for a confrontation. And a part of him still hoped it wasn't true. He wanted to give his best friend the benefit of the doubt—and a chance to change.

He went back out to the living room, trusting that Raymon and Ander would follow. He hoped that Kane would too.

"Okay," Hendrix said when the three of them had gathered around the table with all the clues spread out. "Tell me how this works."

Raymon set down the paper with the image he'd copied from the puzzle. The black light had revealed a whole series of letters, numbers, shapes, and arrows set up in a kind of chart. It reminded Hendrix of the periodic table of elements, only not as easy to understand. Raymon took the pages they'd found and laid them next to the chart.

"I think this matches different clues to each other in sets. And it also has a key to show how they work together." Raymon pointed to a rectangle with a smaller rectangle inside. "See this one? This is the TV screen and the tablet. And these lines inside represent the colors from the TV that helped us get the code."

Hendrix bent over to look at the picture Raymon had copied. "How could we possibly have gotten that from this?" he asked.

"Well," Raymon said, "we couldn't have if we hadn't already solved that clue before we found the puzzle. But it's like a key to show us how to look at the other clues."

Ander rubbed the back of his neck and looked at Hendrix. "I don't get it."

"I'm sorry, Raymon, but I don't either," Hendrix admitted. "I get that one but only because it's already done. I have no idea what the rest of these could be."

"That's what we need to figure out," Raymon said cheerfully. He went back to moving papers around. Every so often he'd ask one of them to go check something or bring him the original clue to look at. He was able to match up the clues for the other two codes they'd already found. After that he didn't seem to be making any progress for a while, but he kept at it with enthusiasm.

"Yes!" he said at last. "The first letters from the words in the commercial, 'green apples bear fruit,' match the music notes G, A, B, and F. When I find those notes on the sheet music from the flight deck it matches the yard lines 50, 20, 30, and 40. If you drop the zeroes you get a code of 5-2-3-4!"

"Let's give it a try," Hendrix said.

The code didn't work on the other door in the hallway, so they went to the door at the bottom of the stairs. Hendrix held his breath as Raymon tapped the code into the keypad. The light flashed green and the door opened.

"I don't get it," Ander said after several long moments.

The room on the other side of the door couldn't really even be called a room. It was more like a metal box. Hendrix finally stepped inside and ran his hand along the smooth, cold surface. He couldn't find a single seam in the floor or the walls, as though the entire thing had been made out of one giant piece of steel.

The sound of laughter brought him back to his senses. Kane stood in the doorway, shaking his head.

"What did I tell you?" he asked. "What. Did. I. Tell. You? It's all just a big trap. End of the line. You're all a bunch of suckers!"

Kane went back up the stairs, still snickering. Hendrix rushed after him and caught up to him in the hallway.

"What is your problem, Kane?" Hendrix snapped.

"My problem is that this whole thing is a big lie. It's a TV show, rigged to make sure we don't win. All they care about is that we put on a good show—get really invested in this, have lots of big emotional moments—and go home with our tails between our legs. And you're giving them exactly what they want."

"Is that why you're working so hard to get us to quit?" Hendrix demanded.

Kane stopped smiling. "I don't know what you mean."

"You've been telling us to give up for hours now. And yet you're still here. Why is that,

Kane? Why would you want us to fail? What's in it for you?"

"I don't . . . That's not what I'm trying to do." He looked away, but not before Hendrix could see shame in his eyes. "I just don't see the point," he finished weakly before walking away.

Hendrix didn't go after him. Now he knew for sure that Kane was lying. But he had no idea why or what to do about it. He couldn't stand the thought of facing that empty room again, so he went back to the living room to see if he could make sense of the chart Raymon had been working on. To his surprise, Kane wasn't back in the den playing *Time Hunters.* Instead, he was sitting on the living room couch, staring off into space.

Raymon and Ander came back upstairs a minute later, looking a little less dazed than they had when Hendrix and Kane left them.

"The room at the bottom of the stairs isn't empty," Raymon said. "I found a secret panel."

Hendrix felt his heart speed up. He remembered the secret compartment in the living room wall. All he had to do was ask

Raymon to show him the trick to getting it to open. Hendrix knew he should have asked him when he first found it, but he'd waited so long that now he was afraid to mention it.

"It's asking for a code," Raymon continued. "But not numbers. This keypad has symbols on it, like the ones we found in the book from the den."

"Which means none of the codes we have now will work on it," Ander added. Then he yawned. "We should get back to work."

Hendrix looked at the countdown clock. Four hours to go. They'd been in the house for eight hours with no sleep, not much to eat, and way too much stress.

"Okay," he said, "but let's split up into pairs. Maybe that will help us focus."

"Works for me," Kane said, shrugging.

"I'll work with you," Raymon told Hendrix. "You worked with Ander earlier while I was working on the puzzle and Kane was playing *Time Hunters*."

"All right," Hendrix agreed. "Is that okay with you, Ander?" He was really asking if

Ander would be okay working with Kane, but Ander just nodded.

Hendrix turned to Raymon. "Four hours to go," he said.

Raymon grinned. "Better get to it then."

CHAPTER
13

"What would we do if this were a video game?" Raymon asked. They were upstairs in the flight deck room where they'd been trying to make sense of the remaining clues on the chart.

"Probably turn it off, vow never to play again, then start over the next day," Hendrix said. They'd all made that threat several times while playing *Time Hunters*. And yet they always found themselves back online, playing as if they'd never doubted they could win.

Raymon nodded. "Let's do that." He caught Hendrix's questioning gaze. "What

I mean is, let's start over. From the very beginning, as if we were coming through the door for the first time. Look at everything as if we hadn't seen it before. Now that we know more about what kinds of things we're looking for, maybe we'll notice something that didn't seem important before."

"Okay," Hendrix said. He didn't really want to waste time retracing their steps, but he didn't have any better ideas.

They went down to the kitchen and stood in the doorway, trying to remember how everything had looked originally. They didn't see anything that matched the symbols they needed, so they moved on. As soon as they walked into the living room, Hendrix saw the wall next to the gadgets. *I should ask Raymon how to get it open*, he thought, feeling guilty.

"I'm sorry," Raymon said before Hendrix had a chance to speak.

"About what?"

Raymon took off his glasses and rubbed at his eyes. "I'm supposed to be the smart one.

I'm supposed to be able to figure this all out, but I can't. I'm letting you down. I'm failing the team."

"Who says . . ." Hendrix had the answer to his question before he even finished asking it. "Did Ms. Pinkney tell you that?"

Raymon nodded. "She said I needed to be extra clever and solve most of the challenges. That's why I insisted on doing that puzzle."

"And it's a good thing you did," Hendrix said, patting him on the shoulder.

"Yeah, but I still can't make it work. So many times I've looked right at something and not been able to figure it out. And then one of you guys does, and I feel like a failure."

Hendrix could have said exactly the same thing. He'd felt like the worst leader since the moment they started. He'd been so busy worrying about what Ms. Pinkney and the studio thought about him that he'd forgotten the point of the game.

"You don't have to be the smart one all the time," Hendrix told Raymon. "Just like I don't have to be the leader."

Raymon looked up, confused. "What do you mean?"

"Ms. Pinkney told me I had to be the leader of the team, that I had to keep everyone on track," Hendrix explained.

Raymon just shook his head in irritation. "I guess we all had roles to play."

Raymon's comment brought Hendrix up short. It was true. He'd been playing a role instead of the game. Clearly Raymon had too. *What roles were Ander and Kane given?* Hendrix thought, thinking through the last eight hours. He remembered the way Ander handed Raymon that code before they'd gotten into the den. How he never seemed to want to share his ideas. The way he'd reacted when Hendrix had apologized for thinking he was just a dumb jock.

And Kane. He'd been working against them from the start. Even before that, when they'd been playing *Time Hunters* at the hotel. Kane was never a cheater, never dishonest or disloyal. He must have been told to act that way.

Hendrix assigned the roles in his head. He was the leader, Raymon was the smart one, Ander was the dumb jock, and Kane was the betrayer.

Everything about his friends' behavior made sense in that light, and Hendrix suddenly felt more confident than he had throughout the whole game. *Those guys were never meant to win this contest*, he thought with determination. *But Hendrix, Raymon, Ander, and Kane are.*

"Raymon," Hendrix said, "can you show me how you got the secret panel to open up in the metal room? I think it might work on this wall too—I'm sure there's a secret panel in it."

Raymon examined the wall for a minute, went to a spot that looked like it was the exact middle, and put his hand against it. A small square pushed back into the wall and then slid down, revealing a cubbyhole with two keys inside.

"How did you know to do that?" Hendrix asked, impressed.

Raymon blushed. "It was luck. I was trying to measure the wall and happened to press there. I only realized it was the center after I'd found it."

Hendrix felt a lot better about not being able to find the compartment himself. It seemed like a lot of the breakthroughs they'd had depended on luck.

"I think this one goes to the kitchen cabinet," Hendrix said, holding up the smaller key. "And the only other door that needs a key is the one in the hallway. Should we try them out or get the others?"

"Let's try them first," Raymon said. "Better to give them good news than false hope."

They went to the kitchen first and were able to get into the cabinet. Inside they found a teapot with symbols all over it.

"I've seen this teapot before!" Raymon said excitedly. "It's on the chart. And these are the same symbols we found in the book from the den. I can use this to decipher the code for the metal room!"

"Let's try the other key first," Hendrix said.

Out in the hallway, Hendrix's hand shook a little as he tried the key. *What are the chances of two big breakthroughs at once? Unless this means we're close to the end?* He hoped that was the case.

The door swung open to reveal another completely empty metal room. Now Hendrix was sure they were close to escaping the house. Raymon tried a couple of walls before finding the secret panel. The keypad inside had the same symbols as the one in the other metal room.

"Do you want me to go figure out the code we just found?" Raymon said.

"Yes, but don't try it out yet," Hendrix said. "All we have left now is to find the codes for the two metal rooms. I want us to do this as a team. There's something I have to do too."

Hendrix went back to the living room to where Kane and Ander were searching.

"Come with me," he said, grabbing Kane and practically pulling him to the bathroom. He shut off both their microphones and looked his best friend straight in the eye. "Tell me the truth. Why are you trying to make us quit or fail?"

Kane blinked a couple of times. "I didn't . . . I didn't want to," he said, looking away. "They told me it was going to be really hard and we probably wouldn't win. But if I got the rest of you to quit then I'd get a bunch of money. I thought, if we weren't going to get the scholarships anyway, I might as well take the cash and run. My dad . . ."

Kane took a deep breath and finally looked at Hendrix. "My dad lost his job a couple of months ago."

"Why didn't you tell me?" Hendrix asked. He couldn't believe Kane hadn't trusted him. Or that he hadn't noticed something was different.

Kane just shrugged. "It's not your problem."

"Hey, that's not true. We're best friends. You were there for me during the worst time in my life," Hendrix reminded him. "Of course I'm going to be there for my best friend when he needs me."

"You mean, we're still friends? Even after this?" Kane's eyes opened wide.

"Come on, man, of course we are." Hendrix

clapped him on the shoulder. "And more than that, we're part of a team. And I don't care what they told you. We're going to win. Or at least, we are if we all work together. What do you say?"

Kane chewed on his lip for a minute. "They won't be happy."

"They want you to be a traitor, right? So go ahead—but betray *them* instead of us."

The wicked grin Hendrix was so used to seeing finally made a reappearance on Kane's face. "They would really hate that, wouldn't they?" Kane snickered. "Let's do it!"

CHAPTER

14

"I'm missing something for this last one," Raymon said a short while later. While he was deciphering the code from the teapot, he'd figured out that there were six other clues that needed to be combined to make three more codes. Since they all used the same kind of symbols, the group had agreed to solve all of the clues before trying the doors.

"Try this," Kane said, pulling a piece of paper out of his pocket and looking ashamed. Since he'd decided to be a real part of the team, he'd been doing his best to make up for lost time. "I should have told you sooner. This pattern of numbers started showing up between levels after I cleared 30."

"You cleared 30 already?" Ander said in amazement. "That's got to be some kind of record."

"It's more than that," Raymon said. "It's exactly what we need. Guys, I've solved the last set of clues. We've got all four codes now. That's everything left on the chart. We have to be close to the end."

"We'd better be," Kane said. "We only have two hours left."

They looked at each other, excited and nervous at the same time.

"Which do we try first?" Hendrix asked. "The hallway or the basement?"

"Hallway's closer," Kane said.

They all raced down the hall and watched as Raymon tapped out the symbols that made the first code he'd found. The light flashed red. But it also had a message that said they keypad was now locked and could be accessed again in fifteen minutes.

"I guess we try downstairs," Hendrix said. The others followed him to the metal room at the bottom of the stairs.

"Should we try the same code or one of the others?" Raymon asked.

They all looked at Hendrix. "The same?" he guessed.

Everyone nodded and Raymon entered the code again. The light flashed red again, but this time the message said they were locked out for 30 minutes.

"If it keeps doubling like that every time we try a code, we won't have enough time to try them all," Ander said.

He was right. The next wrong code would lock them out for one hour, then two hours after that. And they only had two hours left.

"We have to figure out which code and which door on our next two tries," Hendrix concluded.

"No pressure or anything," Raymon said with a nervous laugh.

"Hey," Hendrix said, patting him on the shoulder. "It's not all on you. We need to figure this out as a team."

Raymon nodded and tried to smile. But Hendrix knew he was still feeling the pressure to be what the producers wanted him to be. Hendrix knew because he felt it too.

"We can't do anything down here," Hendrix said. "Let's go back to the living room and check out the codes again."

They all gathered around the table to look at the chart from the puzzle yet again.

"Maybe it has something to do with the order we found the clues in," Kane suggested.

"But we could have found them in a different order," Raymon pointed out.

"Do you have a better idea?" Kane barked. For a minute, Hendrix was afraid he was going to start a fight again. But then Kane took a deep breath and said, "I'm really hoping you do, actually."

"I've got a few theories," Raymon said. "All of the sets of clues on the chart have their own keys or codes. There could be a pattern there. Or it could be as simple as putting the codes into numeric order. But I don't see how that shows us which room belongs to which code."

They all fell silent, studying the chart. But Hendrix was actually studying the other three boys. He was proud of what a great team they'd become, even if it wasn't until the very end. They'd broken free of the roles the studio wanted them to play and . . .

Hendrix noticed Ander's fingers twitching slightly. He turned his head side to side, like he was trying to see the chart from different angles.

"You got something, Ander?" he asked. Hendrix realized that he'd never talked to Ander about his and Raymon's realization. Ander was probably still playing the role of the dumb jock—afraid to share his opinions, to let the world see how smart he really was.

"I think it's a map," he said slowly. "This set of clues is what got us the code to get through the door in the living room," he said, pointing to a spot on the map. "And here is the one for the flight deck. If you imagine a physical map of the house on top of the map of clues, then this would be the code for the metal room off the hallway."

"What about the metal room downstairs?"

Ander pointed to an empty spot on the map. "That room would be here on a map of the house, but there is no code there. And these other three codes"—he pointed to three spots around the edge of the map—"would actually be outside the house. So the fourth code would have to work in that room," he finished confidently.

"How sure are you?" Hendrix asked Ander.

Ander shrugged and bit his lip. But then he pulled his shoulders back and looked Hendrix in the eye. "I'm ninety-five percent sure. My dad's an architect, and I've been looking at blueprints my whole life."

Hendrix realized that, one way or the other, this would be his last act as the leader of this group. If they made the right choice, they won. If they were wrong, they wouldn't have time to try again. They had to get it now. And to be the leader this group needed, he needed to stop being the leader.

"Let's take a vote," he said. "Each person make their case for which code and which room, and then we'll decide together."

Kane argued for his theory, Raymon chose the one he was most certain of, and Ander sketched a map of the house to lay over the clue chart. Hendrix had nothing to contribute, and he was okay with that.

In the end, they all voted for Ander's idea. They had an hour and a half left as they gathered around the door at the end of the hallway for what they hoped was the end of their time in the *Escape!* house.

"Whatever happens," Hendrix said before Ander reached for the keypad, "I'm glad we did this together."

"Me too," the others each said.

They watched as the lockout time ticked down to zero.

Ander entered the code.

CHAPTER

15

"I can't believe it," Kane said for at least the hundredth time in the last hour.

"Well, you're the one who was convinced the whole show was a setup," Hendrix pointed out. "Of course you can't believe we actually won."

They were still on set, filming their post-show interviews. They'd not only managed to get out of the house in time to win the scholarships, they'd gotten out over an hour early. Which meant they each got an extra $10,000 in cash. That was more than the studio had promised Kane if he'd gotten them to all quit.

Even better, because they'd worked out all of the clues on the map, they won a bunch of prizes from the smaller companies sponsoring the show. Now they could keep wearing the designer clothes they'd worn for the contest and use all the products that had been advertised throughout the house.

Kane got to keep the SquarePot NG and the newest edition of *Time Hunters*. None of the other boys were too sad that they didn't get it. As far as Hendrix was concerned, he'd had enough of the game to last a lifetime.

But he had won a TV for figuring out the clue with the colored stripes. Not quite as big as the TV in the *Escape!* house, but big enough that his family would need to rearrange all the furniture in their living room to make it fit. He planned on having a big party to watch their episode of the show when it aired in a few weeks.

Raymon had been awarded a lifetime supply of puzzles, which Hendrix thought was kind of boring, but Raymon seemed happy about it. Ander not only got to keep the tablet he'd used to solve the game, but the studio's architectural firm also offered him an extra scholarship if he decided to study architecture in college and come work for them someday.

The best prize of all, though, was that they were friends again—and better friends than ever. Hendrix noticed that Kane was being extra friendly with Raymon and Ander, taking the time to get to know them and making plans to get together when they got home.

Hendrix also had plans. He was going to use some of his prize money to buy a new viola. And he was going to join the orchestra again as soon as he got back up to speed.

"I'm very proud of you boys," Ms. Pinkney said after they'd finished up their exit interviews.

"But you wanted us to fail." Hendrix said, too tired to keep playing the role of leader.

"Of course, we needed a little controversy to spice things up a bit." Ms. Pinkney smiled sweetly. "But we all knew you'd come through."

Hendrix knew she was lying, but it didn't matter anymore.

"Come on, guys," he said. "Let's go home."

Jannette LaRoche is a librarian in the Quad Cities, Illinois. She has been working with teens for over eighteen years and is passionate about getting the right book into the hands of the right reader at the right time. She is especially interested in connecting teens who don't consider themselves readers with stories that will help them fall in love with books. She holds a BA in English, an MS in library science, and an MFA in creative writing.

REALITY **SHOW**

Escape!
The Island
THE ONE
The Right Note
Treasure Hunt
Warrior Zone

SUDDENLY
ROYAL

**THE VALMONTS ARE NOT YOUR
TYPICAL ROYAL FAMILY.**